D0246280

The Velveteen Rabbit

For all my family. I wouldn't be real without you-SA

For Margery Williams,
to whom I owe a great deal of happiness
thanks to this book, with the greatest respect-RM

A TEMPLAR BOOK

First published in the US in 2011 by Templar Publishing.
This picture book edition published in the UK in 2015 by Templar Publishing,
an imprint of The Templar Company Limited,
Deepdene Lodge, Deepdene Avenue, Dorking, RH5 4AT, UK
www.templarco.co.uk

1 3 5 7 9 10 8 6 4 2

Original edition, 'The Velveteen Rabbit', first published
in the UK in 1922 by William Heinemann Ltd

ISBN 978-1-78370-185-8

Designed by janie louise hunt

Printed in China

The Velveteen Rabbit

By Margery Williams Abridged by Ruth Martin Illustrated by Sophie Allsopp

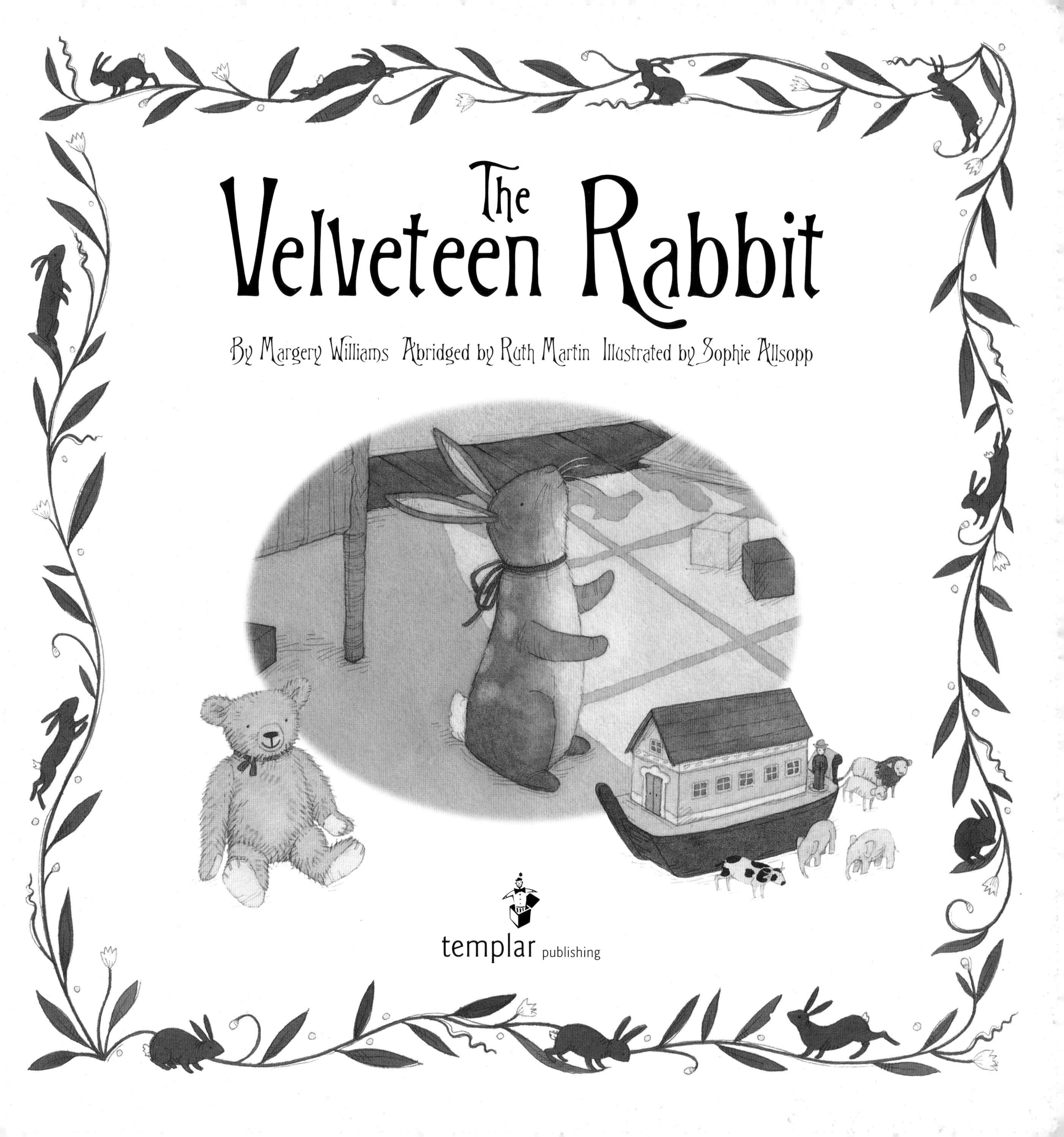

templar publishing

THERE WAS ONCE A VELVETEEN RABBIT, and in the beginning he was really splendid. He was fat and bunchy, as a rabbit should be, and his ears were lined with pink satin.

On Christmas morning, the Velveteen Rabbit sat wedged in the top of the Boy's stocking. For at least two hours, the Boy loved him, but very soon he was forgotten in the excitement of all the new presents. For a long time, no one thought very much about him, and some of the more expensive toys quite snubbed him. The mechanical toys pretended they were Real and looked down upon everyone else. The Rabbit could not claim to be Real, for he didn't know that Real rabbits existed; he thought they were all stuffed with sawdust like himself.

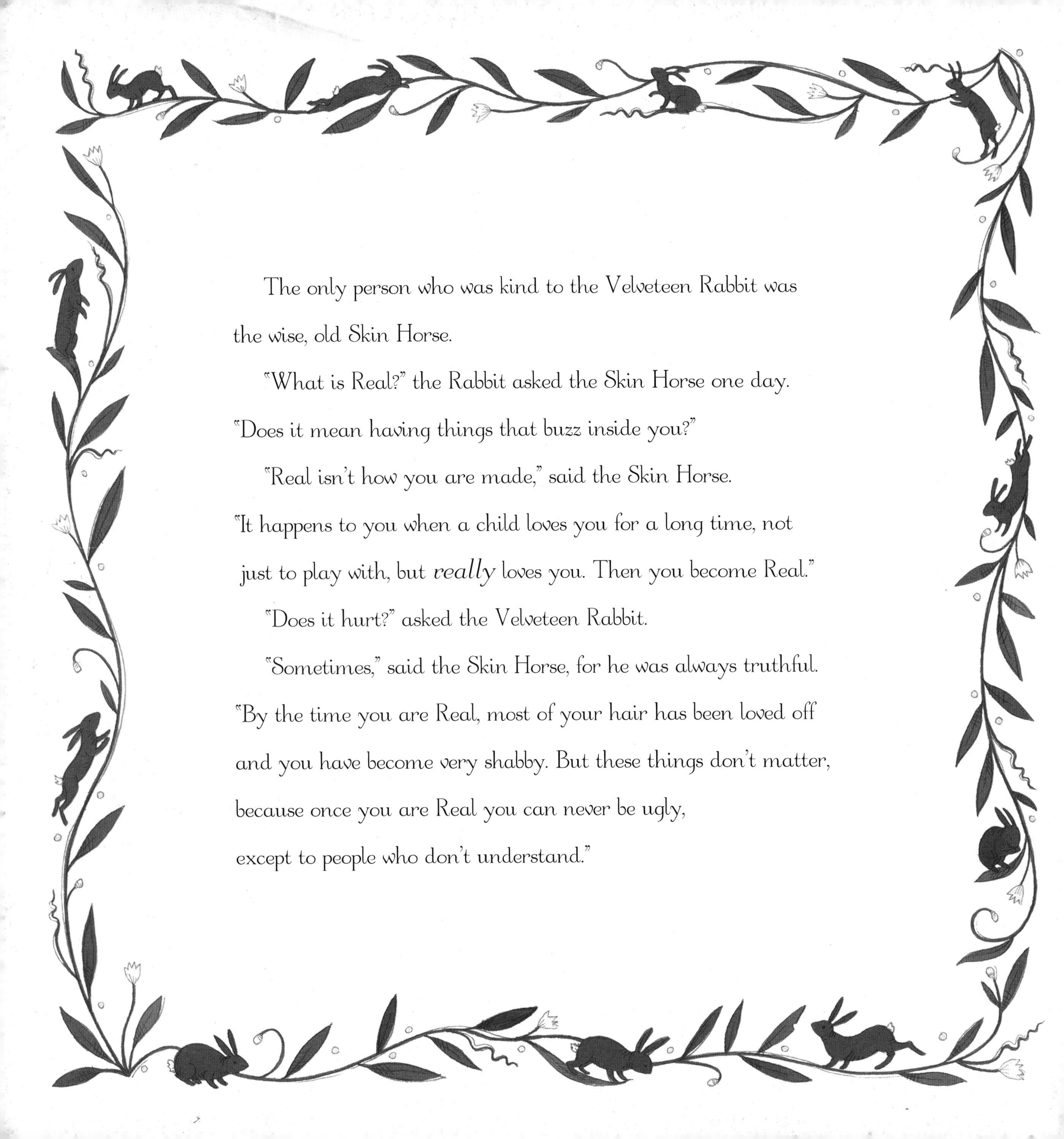

The only person who was kind to the Velveteen Rabbit was the wise, old Skin Horse.

"What is Real?" the Rabbit asked the Skin Horse one day. "Does it mean having things that buzz inside you?"

"Real isn't how you are made," said the Skin Horse. "It happens to you when a child loves you for a long time, not just to play with, but *really* loves you. Then you become Real."

"Does it hurt?" asked the Velveteen Rabbit.

"Sometimes," said the Skin Horse, for he was always truthful. "By the time you are Real, most of your hair has been loved off and you have become very shabby. But these things don't matter, because once you are Real you can never be ugly, except to people who don't understand."

"Are you Real?" asked the Rabbit.

"Yes," said the Skin Horse. "The Boy's uncle made me Real a great many years ago. Once you are Real you can't become unreal again."

The Rabbit sighed. He longed for this magic called Real to happen to him.

There was a person called Nana who ruled the nursery. Sometimes, for no reason whatsoever, she went swooping about like a great wind and hustled the toys away in cupboards. She called this 'tidying up', and the playthings all hated it.

One evening, after Nana had tidied up, the Boy couldn't find the toy dog that always slept with him. Nana was in a hurry, so she simply made a swoop.

"Here," she said, "take your old Bunny! He'll do to sleep with you!"

And so, that night, and for many nights after, the Rabbit slept in the Boy's arms.

He snuggled down, with the Boy's hands clasped round him all night long. As the weeks passed, the Rabbit was so happy that he didn't notice how his fur was getting shabbier, and how the pink had rubbed off his nose where the Boy had kissed him.

Spring came, and they had long days in the garden, for wherever the Boy went, the Rabbit went too. Once, the Rabbit was left out on the lawn until after dusk. Nana was sent to look for him, and as she brought him back, she grumbled, "Fancy all that fuss for a toy!"

The Boy stretched out his hands. "Give me my Bunny!" he said. "You mustn't say that. He isn't a toy. He's REAL!"

When the Velveteen Rabbit heard that, he was happy. The nursery magic had happened to him at last, and he was a toy no longer – he was Real! That night, so much love stirred in his little sawdust heart that it almost burst. Into his boot-button eyes there came a look of wisdom and beauty.

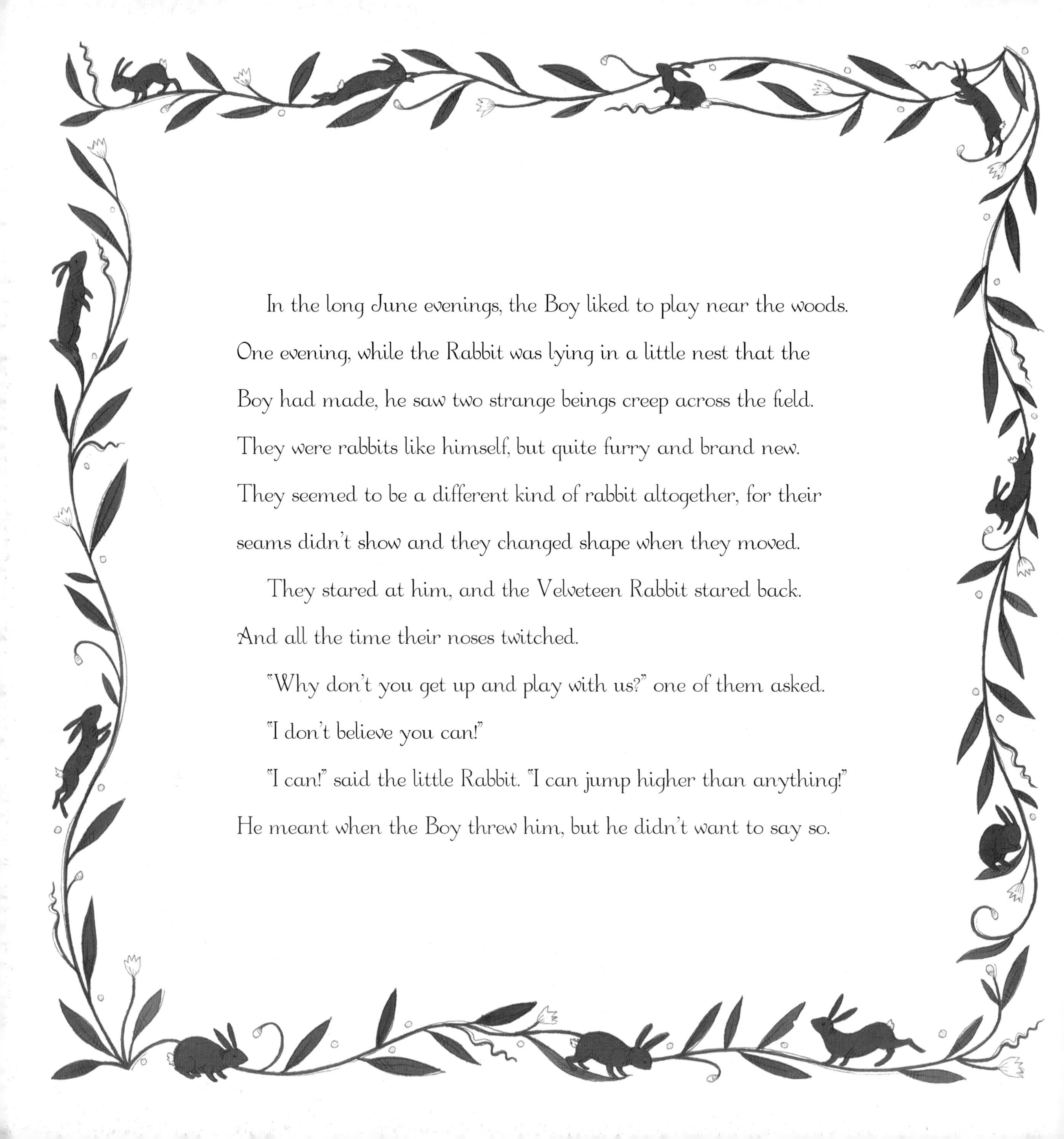

In the long June evenings, the Boy liked to play near the woods. One evening, while the Rabbit was lying in a little nest that the Boy had made, he saw two strange beings creep across the field. They were rabbits like himself, but quite furry and brand new. They seemed to be a different kind of rabbit altogether, for their seams didn't show and they changed shape when they moved.

They stared at him, and the Velveteen Rabbit stared back. And all the time their noses twitched.

"Why don't you get up and play with us?" one of them asked.

"I don't believe you can!"

"I can!" said the little Rabbit. "I can jump higher than anything!" He meant when the Boy threw him, but he didn't want to say so.

"You haven't got any hind legs, have you?" laughed one of the wild rabbits. "If you had you would show them, like this," and he began to whirl round and dance, until the little Rabbit was quite dizzy.

"I have got hind legs. I just don't like dancing," he said. "I'd rather sit still!"

But all the while he was longing to dance, for a funny new tickly feeling ran through him.

"You don't smell right!" sniffed the wild rabbit. "You're not Real!"

"*I am Real!*" said the little Rabbit. "The Boy said so!"

And he nearly began to cry.

He reached for the chocolatey magic
wand on the ground but . . .

It started to run away –
ALL by itself!

The cats were amazed.
"Wow, Keith! You made
it move," they gasped.

Keith was amazed too . . . but he didn't say anything.
"More!" the cats cried, excitedly.
"More magic. More! More!"

Keith took a deep breath.
Then he waved his wand around . . .

“Abracadabra!”

But nothing happened.

Keith tried again.

“Alacazoo!”

Still nothing happened.

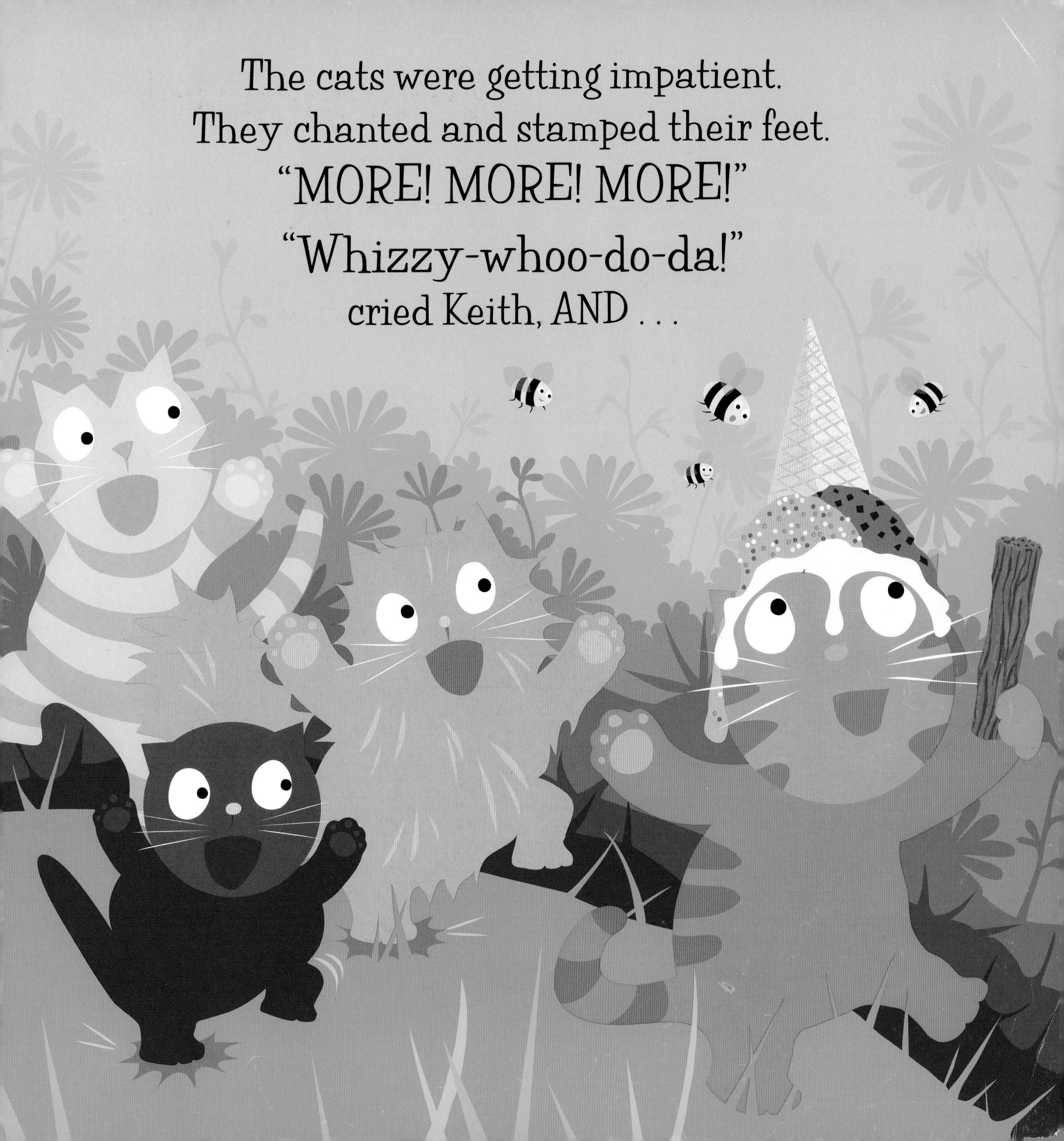

The cats were getting impatient.
They chanted and stamped their feet.
"MORE! MORE! MORE!"
"Whizzy-whoo-do-da!"
cried Keith, AND . . .

. . . just then, a whole family of rabbits popped out of the ground. They'd never heard such a noise!

"Keith – you did it!" the other cats cheered. "You magicked up some rabbits. Hooray!"

They were all having such a fun time that they didn't hear a distant WOOF!

"Yikes! A dog! Quick, Keith, save us with your magic!" the cats squealed in panic.

WOOF! WOOF! WOOF!

But, of course, Keith couldn't REALLY do magic. What was he going to do?

The cats ran up the tree.

They looked down at the barking dog. "Quick, Keith, DO something!" they cried.

Then . . .

Keith's magic hat slipped off his head.
It was falling quickly through the air . . .

PLOP!

"Oh no! Your magic hat!" cried the cats.
"Now you'll NEVER be able to make the dog disappear."

Keith felt terrible.
"It's not a magic hat," he admitted sadly.
"You were right all along – it's just an ice cream, and now we are stuck up this tree FOREVER! I'm sorry!"

But then . . .

BUzZzZZZzzZZzzzz

"Hooray for Keith!" cried the cats.
"You're magic even without your hat!"
"Thank you," said Keith shyly. "And, for my next trick, I will make this blob of ice cream on the end of my nose disappear."

The cats waited patiently.

Then . . .

Keith stuck out his tongue and licked it off!